# I Wish I Had Glasses Like Rosa
## Quisiera tener lentes como Rosa

Written by / Escrito por Kathryn Heling and Deborah Hembrook
Illustrated by / Ilustrado por Bonnie Adamson

*To all my little kindergarten friends with glasses, especially Kat!*
*—Love from Mrs. Hembrook*
*XO*

*To Joshua and Amy, best friends!*
*—KEH*

*To Jenny and Steffie, always, glasses or not!*
*—BCA*

Text Copyright © 2007 Kathryn Heling and Deborah Hembrook
Illustration Copyright © 2007 Bonnie Adamson
Translation Copyright © 2007  Raven Tree Press

All rights reserved.  For information about permission to reproduce selections from this book, write to: Permissions,
Raven Tree Press, a Division of Delta Systems Co., Inc., 1400 Miller Parkway, McHenry IL 60050.  www.raventreepress.com

Heling, Kathryn and Hembrook, Deborah.


I wish I had glasses like Rosa/written by Kathryn Heling and Deborah Hembrook; illustrated by Bonnie Adamson;
translated by Eida de la Vega = Quisiera tener lentes como Rosa/escrito por Katheryn Heling y Deborah Hembrook;
ilustrado por Bonnie Adamson; traducción al español de Eida de la Vega.—1st ed.—McHenry, IL: Raven Tree Press, 2007.

    p. ; cm.

Bilingual Text in English and Spanish or English only editions

Summary: Abby goes to elaborate and comical lengths to get glasses like Rosa.
      She realizes she might have something that is just as desirable as the
      longed–for glasses. Abby gains appreciation of her own uniqueness.

Bilingual Version           English Only Version
ISBN: 978-0-9724973-3-4 Hardcover    ISBN: 978-1-934960-48-6 Hardcover
ISBN: 978-0-9770906-5-5 Paperback    ISBN: 978-1-934960-49-3 Paperback

1. Eyeglasses—Juvenile Fiction. 2. Individuality—Juvenile Fiction. 3. Self–Esteem—Juvenile Fiction. 4. Bilingual books—
English and Spanish. 5. [Spanish language materials—books.] I. Heling, Kathryn and Hembrook, Deborah. II. Adamson,
Bonnie, ill. III. Vega, Eida de la. IV. Title. V. Title: Quisiera tener lentes como Rosa.

      PZ73.H38345 2007        LCCN—2006014022

      [E]—dc22          CIP

Printed in Taiwan
10 9 8 7 6 5 4 3 2
first edition

**Free activities for this book are available at www.raventreepress.com**

# I Wish I Had Glasses Like Rosa
## Quisiera tener lentes como Rosa

Written by / Escrito por Kathryn Heling and Deborah Hembrook

Illustrated by / Ilustrado por Bonnie Adamson

Raven Tree Press
A Division of Delta Systems Co., Inc.
www.raventreepress.com

I wish I had glasses like Rosa.
They make her look beautiful!

Quisiera tener lentes como Rosa.
¡Se ve muy bonita con ellos!

Rosa and I like to build.
We wear safety glasses.
I love wearing glasses!

A Rosa y a mí nos gusta construir cosas.
Usamos lentes de protección.
¡Me encanta usar lentes!

One morning, I wore my grandma's reading glasses.
Everything looked funny.

Una mañana, me puse los lentes de leer de mi abuela.
Todo se veía rarísimo.

Then they slipped off my nose.
I'll never do that again!

Se me deslizaron por la nariz.
¡No lo volveré a hacer jamás!

When I swim, I wear goggles.
I pretend they're real glasses.

Cuando nado, uso lentes de nadar
y me hago la idea de que son lentes de verdad.

I wear them on the beach, too.

También los uso en la playa.

15

16

In art class, I made glasses out of clay.
They were perfect.

En la clase de arte, hice unos lentes de plastilina.
Me quedaron perfectos.

Then they drooped.
I'll never do that again!

Pero se aflojaron enseguida.
¡No lo volveré a hacer jamás!

19

I found the glasses my dad wore for a party.

Me encontré los lentes que mi papá usó en una fiesta.

They made my nose itch.
Dad said I needed a shave.

Me hacían cosquillas en la nariz.
Papá dijo que me vendría bien un afeitado.

23

At recess, I wore my eyeball glasses.

En el recreo, me puse unos lentes con los ojos colgando.

The eyeballs bounced when I jumped rope.
I'll never do that again!

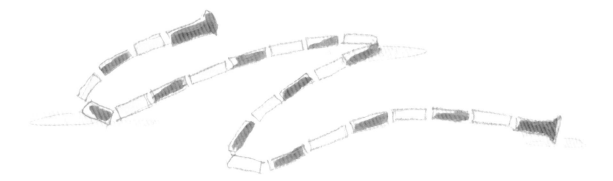

Los ojos brincaban cada vez que yo saltaba la suiza.
¡No lo volveré a hacer jamás!

27

I still wish I had glasses
like Rosa!
But Rosa wishes she had
freckles like me!

Todavía quiero tener lentes
como Rosa.
¡Sin embargo, Rosa quiere
tener pecas como yo!

Imagine that!

¡Imagínate!

# Vocabulary
## English

glasses

beautiful

nose

swim

beach

art class

Dad

party

jump

imagine

# Vocabulario
## Español

los lentes

bonita

la nariz

nado (nadar)

la playa

la clase de arte

el papá

la fiesta

saltaba (saltar)

imagínate (imaginar)